HOPELESS HEROES

HERA'S TERRIBLE TRAP!

Sweet Cherry
PUBLISHING

STELLA TARAKSON

Published by Sweet Cherry Publishing Limited
Unit 36, Vulcan House,
Vulcan Road,
Leicester, LE5 3EF
United Kingdom

First published in the US in 2019
2019 edition

2 4 6 8 10 9 7 5 3 1

ISBN: 978-1-78226-551-1

© Stella Tarakson

Hopeless Heroes: Hera's Terrible Trap!

Cover design by Nick Roberts and Rhiannon Izard
Illustrations by Nick Roberts

www.sweetcherrypublishing.com

Printed and bound in India
I.TP002

*In memory of my mother, Helen, a migrant
who brought her mythology with her*

1

Tim Baker wrapped his scarf around his neck. It was unusually cold for May. The clouds were heavy with rain despite the fine weather forecast. As if defying the television weatherperson, a splatter of rain plonked firmly onto Tim's forehead and slithered down his nose.

He shuddered.

There were plenty of other things he'd rather be doing on a soggy Sunday

morning. Like playing computer games
in his cozy living room. Or chatting with
his best friend, Ajay. Or even – yep – *even*
finishing off his math homework. But no.
He couldn't do any of those things. Tim
fished a damp tissue out of his pocket and
blew his nose glumly.

An outdoor garden center! Of all things! Row after row of nothing but leaves, stems and petals. And a whole bunch of adults in raincoats nodding and making *ooh* and *ah* sounds, as if they'd never seen a plant before. Really, didn't they have anything better to do with their time?

Not that there was anything amazing waiting for him at home, Tim realized, a lump forming in his throat. Not since his good friend Hercules had left.

Tim's adventures had started when he accidentally broke an Ancient Greek vase his mother owned. Incredibly, an enormous figure had erupted out through the cracks. At first Tim thought he'd released a genie. Instead it turned out to be the hero Hercules. Half human, half god, Hercules was the son of a mortal woman and Zeus, king of the Olympian gods. Not what you normally find in a vase, but since then Tim had learned to expect the unexpected.

Hercules had been trapped in the vase thousands of years ago by Hera, Zeus' wife. The queen goddess was jealous of Hercules' beautiful mother. From the moment the demigod was born, Hera had decided to hate and resent him. If it hadn't been for Tim's accident, the hero would still be in the vase now, perched on the mantelpiece, a terrible secret trapped forever.

"Come along, dear, keep up," Tim's mother said as she strode past some hyacinths.

"Can we go home now?" Tim asked, picking up his pace.

"Not yet."

"But it's cold." He glanced at the sky. "And it's starting to rain."

Mom muttered something under her breath and kept walking.

Tim tried again. "I'm bored."

Mom turned and fixed Tim with a penetrating stare. "We wouldn't be here at all, if it weren't for … well, you know why." She pressed her lips together and put a tray of petunias in her cart.

Mom didn't say it out loud but Tim knew what she meant. If he hadn't destroyed their garden, she wouldn't need to replant it. Except … he hadn't been the one to slash and burn all their flowers. It had been Hercules.

Asking the hero for help with the weeding had turned out to be a big mistake. How was Tim to know that Hercules thought plants had to be fought off like the Hydra, a multi-headed monster whose heads grew back after being sliced off? Hercules was super-strong but not exactly super-smart. Even so, he'd proved to be a loyal friend. He had sided with him against Leo the bully, and encouraged Tim to stand up for himself. Despite all the trouble he'd caused at home and at school, Tim missed Hercules. There had been no such thing as boredom when the hero was around.

Unlike now.

Sighing, Tim trailed after his mother as she turned yet another corner.

And fell flat on his face.

Malicious laughter erupted above him. Tim looked up to see his worst enemy, Leo, looming over him, a grin on his flushed face.

"OOPS! CLUMSY."

Leo snickered.

Tim knew very well that he'd been tripped on purpose. He pulled himself to his feet with as much dignity as he could muster.

"What are you doing here, Cinderella?"

Leo used the nickname that he'd made up. It was a cruel dig at the fact that Tim did housework. Not that he wanted to, of course, but Mom worked two jobs and he had to help out. That didn't stop the bully from teasing him about it, however.

"Having fun looking at the flowers, are you? Find anything nice?" Leo pursed his lips in a mock pout and fluttered his eyelashes.

Was it worth pointing out that Leo was at the garden center too? Tim paused, pondering the best way to put this.

The bully must have misinterpreted

Tim's thoughtful expression for one of fear.

"Go on, go find your mommy," Leo sneered. "Maybe she'll buy you a pretty flower so you won't cry."

Normally Tim would walk away, preferring to avoid trouble rather than tackle it head-on. But since he'd outsmarted Leo once before, he'd grown bolder in their encounters.

"Yeah, I'm just chilling." Tim folded his arms and ignored the dirt and dead leaves clinging to his pants. "But why are *you* here? Have you suddenly become a botanist?"

Leo narrowed his eyes and didn't answer. Tim suspected the bully was

trying to work out what a botanist was,
and whether he'd just been insulted.
Shrugging, Leo pulled a bag of jelly beans
out of his pocket and popped a red one
into his mouth.

Tim's stomach growled at the sight of the food. He hadn't eaten since breakfast and it was nearly lunchtime. He clamped a hand over his gut, hoping Leo hadn't heard.

"Ooh, would ya like one?" Leo patted the bulging bag. "Sorry, I'm all out."

"Leo! Where've you got to? Leo!"

The angry voice grew louder. Tim saw a small woman striding toward them, her head darting from side to side like a bird of prey. Her gray hair was pulled back in a severe bun and her eyes flashed behind thick glasses.

"Here, Grandma," Leo called out half-heartedly. He dropped his gaze to the ground.

"Where? Drat the boy. Always wandering off. One of these days I'll …"

"I said here!" Leo turned toward the small figure, a look of misery on his face. "You're lucky I'm busy," he shot over his shoulder at Tim. "Otherwise I'd slug you."

Tim hesitated – but only for a moment. Just as Leo started to walk away, Tim put his foot out.

"Oops! Clumsy." Tim repeated Leo's excuse as the bully fell face first into the dirt.

Leo grunted as he hit the ground, hard.
Tim darted off before the bully had
a chance to pull himself upright, the
words "I'll get you for that, Cinderella!"
ringing in his ears.

Tim realized that giving Leo a taste
of his own medicine probably wasn't the
smartest thing to do, but he knew that
Hercules would have been proud. Acting
quickly, Tim thrust himself into a group

of chattering old ladies clustered around
a stand of waving sunflowers. Leo would
think twice about following him into their
midst, especially with his grandma watching.

Concerned about drawing attention to himself, Tim tried to look interested in the display.

It was the first time he'd ever seen a sunflower up close. Something caught his eye. Its bright yellow head was filled with pointy little seeds. Tim had eaten sunflower seeds many times before as a snack, but had never been bored enough to give them much

thought. But now – safe from Leo and with Mom still shopping – he had plenty of time to kill. He peered at the blossom. How exactly did the seeds come out? Did they fall when you shook them? Experimenting, Tim grasped the flower's long stalk and shook it gingerly.

Nothing happened.

He tried a bit harder.

Still nothing.

And a little bit harder …

"Hey! Whaddya think you're doing?"

The voice of a store assistant took Tim by surprise. Startled, he jerked back, snapping the stem clean through.

"YOU CAN'T DO THAT!"

The assistant started
wading through the
crowd of shoppers in Tim's
direction, an angry look on
his face.

With the sunflower still in
his hand, Tim ran the opposite
way. Any minute now the
assistant might call the police

– and then he'd really be in trouble. They wouldn't believe it was an accident. They'd think he was a vandal. Or a thief. Quick, he had to hide the evidence! Panting, Tim scrunched the flower up in his palm and shoved it in his pants pocket.

"Tim! There you are. Slow down!" Mom wheeled her laden cart over to him and put her hand on his shoulder. "Where did you vanish to?"

"Mom. Can we go now? Please." He tried not to sound frantic.

Mom looked Tim up and down, taking in his wild expression and heaving chest.

"What's up?"

"Nothing. I–"

"Madam, your son has been damaging

store property." The assistant caught up with them, huffing and puffing, his face redder than the store's roses. He was carrying the pot with the decapitated sunflower.

"Why? What did he do?" Mom gripped Tim's shoulder harder than was necessary.

"This." The assistant hoisted up the plant. "I'm afraid you'll have to buy it."

Mom looked like she was about to argue, but then changed her mind. "Yes, all right. I'm sorry about that. I'm sure it was an accident."

The assistant sniffed in disbelief and plunked the severed plant into Mom's cart. He glared at Tim, then flounced away.

"Would you care to explain that, Timothy?" Mom asked as they got in line for the register. She only called him Timothy when she was angry.

"It was an accident! I was just looking at it. I didn't mean to break it."

"What is it with you and flowers?"

Tim didn't know what to say.

"At least you didn't set fire to anything," she said wryly. Tim couldn't tell whether she was joking or not. "Come on, help me unload the cart. When we get home I'll make us some lunch. Spaghetti okay?"

Tim's gurgling stomach answered for him.

■ ■ ■

Mom bustled around the kitchen,

cooking and humming a cheerful tune. She'd been in a good mood ever since a publisher had accepted her book – which was probably why Tim wasn't in trouble for breaking the sunflower. Thankfully she'd believed him when he'd said it was an accident. Mom had been busier than ever lately, but she was happy and that made her nicer. Most of the time.

Tugging off his rain-spattered coat, Tim ran into his bedroom to check on the vase. Hercules ought to be happy too, he thought, now that he finally had what he wanted. By solving a tricky riddle printed on the vase, Tim had been able to send the demigod back to his family in Ancient Greece.

For the third time that day, Tim made sure that the vase was still in his wardrobe. He whipped off the sheet that cloaked it and there it was, its fracture lines visible even in the gloomy light. A few days ago Tim had removed the glued-together vase from the living room mantelpiece and put it where he could keep a close eye on it. Mom didn't seem to mind.

Although he didn't say why, Tim had a very good reason for wanting to keep the vase hidden. Not long after Hercules had left, two intruders had entered Tim's house in the dead of night. They had tried to steal the vase from right under Tim's horrified gaze.

One was the evil goddess Hera, who wanted to use the vase to recapture Hercules. The other intruder was her servant, a young man called Hermes. He had wings on his cap and sandals and used them to fly. Hermes was clearly terrified of Hera, which only reinforced all of the awful things Hercules had said about her.

Tim had managed to stop them from taking the vase, but the flying guy had threatened to return. Tim kept his gaze on the big black vessel as he started to unknot his scarf. Hermes and Hera could come back at any—

"Hey!" Tim yelped, his eyes bulging.

The vase! It was floating!

At first it looked like there was
nobody holding it, but Hermes gradually
materialized. His body shimmered as
it solidified in front of Tim's eyes. The
intruder's gaze sharpened when he saw
Tim watching him.

"Got it!" Hermes crowed. "Sweet. Hera
will be delighted." The wings on his cap and
sandals started to flap vigorously

and he rose into the air. "So long, pal!"

"No-o-o-o!" Without thinking, Tim rushed at the flying figure. He jumped, hands outstretched, and hooked his fingers around the handles.

"HAH!"

But Tim's shout of triumph turned to a cry of fear as he felt himself being lifted off his feet. Higher and higher they went. He was flying! Soon he'd hit the ceiling. Except, somehow they went through it … A shower of golden sparks danced around his body, thick and fast, blinding him.

Tim shut his eyes and clung on for dear life.

Tim felt himself swirling through the air at great speed. The wind shrieked and gibbered as it spun him left and right, up and down, round and round. It was surprisingly warm, rather like being buffeted by a giant tumble dryer. Although it wasn't painful, his arms and legs went numb. It took all his strength to keep a grip on the vase's handles. Building up his courage, Tim opened one eye. All he could see was an impenetrable golden mist. He couldn't see Hermes or the vase, or even his own body. Better to keep his eyes firmly shut, Tim decided, and hope things would return to normal soon.

After just a few minutes he felt himself land. The ground was wonderfully firm and stable beneath his feet. Sensation returned to his arms and legs. Was he still in his bedroom? Tim took a moment to steady himself, then snapped open his eyes.

Hermes was standing in front of him, still holding on to the vase. The wings on his cap fluttered slowly and came to a halt.

"Hera won't like this," he said grimly. "Still, not my problem. I did what she said."

"What happened?
Where—"

"You can let go of the vase
now." Hermes tugged as he
spoke. "I said, you can let … go …"
With a great heave he pulled it out of
Tim's grasp. "That's better."

Tim looked around in disbelief. He
wasn't in his bedroom. Instead, he was
standing in a majestic courtyard lined
with soaring white columns and leafy
palms. The floor was paved with giant
slabs of limestone, which glittered in the
bright sunlight. At the other end of the
courtyard was an Ancient Greek temple.
It looked a lot like the pictures of ruins
that Tim had seen in books, except this

one was intact. It had a shallow triangular roof with bright red and blue decorations.

Tim wondered whether he was hallucinating. Maybe he'd passed out from garden center boredom and was now dreaming. It was possible. Nothing else made sense.

"I wouldn't stand about gawking if I were you," Hermes said, his golden curls catching the light and glowing like sunflower petals. "You know what to do?"

Tim blinked. "Wake up?"

"No." Hermes looked bemused. "Run. Now."

"But – but … What? Where?"

Hermes sighed. "Need it spelled out, do you? Hmm. And Hercules said you were bright."

"I–"

He rolled his eyes. "Right. I'm Hermes, the messenger god. Nice to meet you." His wings flapped in greeting. "I serve the queen goddess Hera. And this is her temple." He spoke slowly, stressing every word, as if Tim were dim-witted. "Hera wanted her vase back. I got it for her. You're in danger. End of story."

The god was very different from when he'd first broken into Tim's house. Then he had bumbled and stumbled and seemed utterly terrified of Hera. Now he was calm and cool and in control. Tim suspected that was because Hera was not around to yell at him.

"So … I'm in Ancient Greece? I'm not dreaming?"

Hermes rolled his eyes. "You're in Greece," he agreed. "In Hera's courtyard. So run!"

"But where do I go? How will I get home?"

It was all too much to take in.

"What part of the word 'run' don't you understand? Figure it out later, kid. Just go before it's too late."

An angry snarling, yowling sound filled the air. It sounded like a cross between dogs barking and a nightmarish scream.

"Oops," Hermes said, leaning casually against a column. "Too late."

The yowling grew louder. It made Tim's blood run cold. Before he could take a step, a flock of large blue birds rushed into the courtyard. Spotting him, they squawked and fanned out their shiny tail feathers. It looked as if hundreds of bright eyes were glaring at him as their tail feathers shook and glistened. Tim stared at them, his mouth hanging open.

Peacocks.

He was about to be mobbed by a gang of peacocks. And he'd thought things couldn't get any stranger. Growling like guard dogs, the birds circled around Tim, cutting off his retreat.

"What's wrong, my petals? What's upsetting you?" a velvety voice cooed as a tall, thin woman approached.

Tim recognized the goddess Hera. He tried to back away but bumped against a beak.

"WHO ARE YOU?"

she demanded, her voice as icy as her eyes. She raised a hand and the birds fell silent.

"This is Tim Baker, Your Majesty," Hermes said, bowing. The tinge of fear had entered his voice again.

"What?! How did he get here?" She glared at Tim as if he were something nasty that she'd scraped off her sandal.

"Forgive me, Your Majesty. It wasn't my fault. He hitched a ride. I couldn't shake him off." Hermes bowed so low that his forehead nearly touched the floor.

"Tim. Tim. What sort of name is Tim?" Hera said scornfully, striding toward him. "It sounds like a plate cracking."

"It's short for Timothy," Tim said, pulling himself up to his full height.

Hera curled her lip. "Is it indeed? Do you know what Timothy means?"

Tim shrugged. He'd never really thought about it.

"It's a Greek name. It means 'honoring god'. I am a god. So honor me!" She flung her arms out to the side and spun in a slow circle.

Tim had no idea what she was babbling about. His glance slid to Hermes, who was wringing his hands and averting his gaze. What

did this crazy woman want Tim to do?
Pray to her?

A thoughtful look crossed the goddess'
face. She came to a standstill.

"There is something you can do to show
me that honor, my child." Her voice was
as silky as when she spoke to her birds.
"The fool Hercules walks the streets.
He trusts you. Help me trap him in this
vase, and you will share in the riches
of Mount Olympus. I will make you a
god!" She sashayed up to Tim and rested
a bony hand on his shoulder. Her smile
was exaggerated and unnatural, as if she
hadn't had much practice.

Tim recoiled. "No." If being a god
meant living in fear like Hermes, he'd

41

rather be an ordinary boy. "Hercules is my friend and I won't hurt him. He told me all about you!"

Hera's already pale face turned as white as marble. "Then I shall trap you too!"

Her pretence at friendliness hadn't lasted long. Hera reached out to grab him, and Tim finally took Hermes' advice.

He ran.

Heart pounding, Tim darted between two columns, then ran down a flight of stone steps. He could hear the yowling of the peacocks as they bustled after him. Tim ran faster. Head down, feet flying, arms flailing, running blindly. He hit a tall solid object that stopped him in his tracks.

"Watch where you're going," a deep voice growled. "You nearly made me drop my honey cake."

The voice was wonderfully familiar. Tim
looked up into the angry eyes of the man
he had collided with.

"HERCULES?"

"Tim Baker! It cannot be! What are you doing here, my friend?" Hercules scooped Tim up into the air, a giant grin lighting up his face. "Have you missed me? I've missed you, too. Did you come to meet my family and try some of this magnificent cake? You are most welcome!"

"Thanks, but that's not … I mean I … oh, help!"

"Help you what?"

Tim pointed a trembling arm. They had to get away quickly, before they were captured by the angry goddess.

"Hera–"

Hercules sniffed. "I'm not inviting her to lunch. Not after what she did to me. But come, my wife shall prepare us the finest feast in all of Greece." Tucking Tim under his armpit, the hero strode down the street. He hummed happily as he bit into his syrupy cake. The sound of peacocks faded into the distance and Tim slumped with relief. Now that he was safe, he was starting to feel hungry. The thought of a feast was very welcome.

"Here we are," Hercules said after a few minutes of rapid walking. He ducked under the doorway of an imposing two-story house. They entered straight into an open courtyard, around which the house was built. "Agatha!"

A woman came out through a doorway. She was dressed in a simple blue ankle-length chiton with a silky band knotted around her waist. Her fair hair was braided and wrapped on top of her head.

"My love, this is Tim Baker, the boy who broke the vase. He's come for a visit."

"Put him down, dear." Hercules' wife had a gentle voice and serene face. "He looks upset."

"That's because—" Tim started.

"ZOE!"

Hercules bellowed. He carried Tim inside and set him down on a woven rug. "Come meet a friend."

Scampering footsteps rushed toward them. A small figure burst into the room, dressed in a bright red chiton. Despite her diminutive size, Zoe looked about Tim's age. Like her father, she had warm brown eyes and black curly hair. But instead of sitting neatly against her head, her curls exploded in a frenzy of wild ringlets that showered down her back.

"This is—" Hercules began.

"The boy from the future! I can tell from his strange clothes." Zoe's eyes shone and she turned to Tim eagerly. "What's it like where you're from? Do kids have adventures? Can girls go to school? Are fathers still so bossy?"

"Slow down. Both of you." Agatha fixed her family with a firm stare. "The boy looks exhausted. He could do with a rest and a good meal. After that, he can tell us how he came to be here and what's upsetting him. Sit down, young man."

She turned and walked through the doorway.

"Zoe, come with me. We'll get him something to eat."

"Yes, Ma," Zoe called after her, but she stayed where she was. "So, tell me. What *is* it like in the future?" Her head tilted to the side like an inquisitive sparrow.

Tim didn't know where to begin. How could he explain thousands of years of change in just a few sentences?

"Err … um … it's good. Didn't your dad tell you about it?" Hercules had been there long enough, surely, to describe the modern world to his family.

"Oh, he never tells me anything. He thinks girls should stay home and not do anything exciting." Zoe's eyes slid to her father, who flashed her a severe look.

"Excitement can be dangerous," Hercules said, folding his arms. "If you don't know that yet, then it is best you remain in the house."

"Zoe, where are you?' Agatha called. "I asked you to come."

"Dad, could you please help Ma with lunch?"

"What?" Hercules boomed, making the walls vibrate. "You want me to prepare food, like a woman?"

"Yes, please." Zoe sparkled at her father.

"Well, all right then! Just checking." And Hercules strode purposefully from the room.

"He's sweet," Zoe said, a smile flitting across her face. "But he won't let me do anything or go anywhere on my own."

Tim hadn't forgotten how Hercules

had kept trying to protect him from dangers that didn't exist. It had been a bit stressful at the time. After the hero had left, however, Tim felt lonelier than he had since his father died. "Yeah. He was like that with me, too."

"Even though you're a boy? Gosh, I've got no chance!"

Tim shrugged. "You should be glad you've got a father who cares so much."

"I know. I am, really." A look of genuine affection lit Zoe's face. "But the thing is, he's the one that needs protecting, not me. I'm smart enough to avoid danger, but Dad walks right into it. Like the way he got trapped in the vase! He didn't see that coming. Ma warned him to stay away from

Hera, but …" Zoe shook her head.

"How did it happen? How was he caught?"

"I don't know. He won't tell me." Zoe sighed. "At least it's over. The vase is in your home, out of Hera's reach."

Tim shuffled his feet. "Not exactly."

"What do you mean?"

Tim told the girl how the vase was stolen and taken to Hera's temple, with him attached. He explained that Hera threatened to capture him because he wouldn't agree to trick Hercules. "I managed to escape, but had to leave the vase behind. I – I'm sorry. I think Hera's going to use the vase to try to catch your dad again."

Zoe's face turned white.

"We need to get the vase back. Now."
She didn't waste her words.

"But – but how?" Tim spluttered, taken
by surprise. "It's too dangerous. We'll get
caught. And anyway, will your dad let us
go?"

"I'm not going to ask him."

"Can't we eat first?" Tim asked. He liked
the idea of an Ancient Greek feast and
could feel another tummy rumble building
up.

"Don't be silly. Come on, we're wasting
time."

Zoe turned and hurried out the front
door. Tim watched her helplessly for a
moment. He couldn't let her just walk into

danger like that. Didn't she know the risks she faced? Zoe might be brave and smart, but could she stand up against Hera? Now Tim understood why Hercules fretted so much when he was away from his family.

"Hey, wait for me!" Tim called.

Without a backward glance, he ran outside and chased after the fleeing figure.

"There's no one here," Zoe said as they approached Hera's temple. "See? Empty."

Eyes darting from side to side, Tim followed close on her heels. "Maybe. But we'd better hurry. She might be back any minute."

"Did you see where they put the vase?" Zoe asked, but Tim shook his head. "Let's try inside," she said, bounding up the steps.

They entered the dim inner chamber.

Tim came to a halt when he saw a larger-than-life statue of Hera, right in the center. Made of gold and ivory, the goddess was sitting on a gigantic throne. She had a scepter in one hand and a pomegranate in the other. The statue appeared to be glaring right at him.

"Do you think she can see us?" he whispered, reluctant to get any nearer.

"Don't be silly," Zoe laughed. Then she looked at him curiously. "Why do you ask? In your world, can statues see?"

"No, of course not. They're made of stone."

"Well, come on then." Zoe tossed her curls over her shoulder. "Let's try the antechamber."

Tim let the girl lead him past the glaring Hera toward an area that was piled high with offerings. Coins, weapons, jewelry, ornate pots. Tim couldn't believe that so many people had left gifts to the goddess.

"There it is!" Tim exclaimed. The vase stood on a low marble plinth, almost hidden among the jumble. "Quick, let's grab it and go."

"Hang on a second." Zoe circled around the plinth and stared at the back of the vase. "What's this say?" She was looking at the Ancient Greek writing that Tim had had so much trouble translating. He knew that part of it was the spell that allowed him to send Hercules back home.

"Did your dad tell you about the riddle?"
Tim asked. "How I solved it for him?"

Zoe nodded, her eyes glued to the vase.

"That's what some of it says. I don't
know the rest. Your dad wouldn't say.
Maybe he couldn't read it, or maybe
he didn't want me to know. I got the
feeling he wanted to keep it a secret."
Tim scratched his head. "I reckon it's
important, though. I tried to get someone
who can read it, but …"

"*I* can read it."

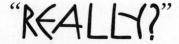

Tim couldn't disguise the doubt in his
voice.

"Whaddya mean? Yes, really!"

Tim raised his eyebrows. Since meeting Hercules, he'd been reading about life in Ancient Greece. He knew that girls didn't go to school. They stayed home with their mothers and learned to cook and weave.

"Mom taught me," Zoe said defensively. "She's very smart, you know. Not like Dad," she added under her breath. "Get out of my way. It says … right, here's the bit about the riddle. And this part says … Mmm."

"We should hurry. Hera might return." Tim plucked at Zoe's chiton. "You can read it at home."

"No chance." Zoe snorted. "Dad'll confiscate it, and then we'll never know. Now, let me concentrate. These are all different spells, did you know that? This line says, *'Those who hold me understand and are understood.'* She looked up. "What does that mean?"

Tim frowned for a moment then his brow cleared. "You speak Greek, right? And I speak English. But I've held the vase, so that explains how we can talk to each other."

"Humph." Zoe didn't look pleased that Tim had figured out the answer before she did. "Then what about this? *'Those who hold me, command me.'* Command it to do what?"

Before Tim had a chance to think what that could mean, angry cries filled the air.

THE PEACOCKS!

Dozens of them fluttered into the antechamber, then charged at Tim and Zoe. Within seconds, they were surrounded by the furious squawking birds.

"Quick, grab it and run!" Tim shouted.

"Too late, I'm afraid." Hera's voice cut across the temple as she sashayed toward them. "You don't think I'm foolish enough to leave the vase unguarded? Silly children!"

"So what are you going to do about it?" Zoe asked, hands on her hips. The fierce look in her eyes was just like her father's when he encountered a foe.

Hera lifted a hand to her chin and

paused, as if thinking. "Well now, let me
see. How about … this?" she said, and
clicked her fingers.

Suddenly everything changed. Tim
and Zoe were no longer standing in the
crowded antechamber. Instead, they

were in a long narrow corridor with soaring walls and a solid floor. The birds, the offerings, the vase and Hera had all disappeared.

"What happened? Where are we?"

Tim ran to the end of the corridor, only to be confronted by another high wall and another long corridor. Turning, he dashed to the other end. It was exactly the same.

"No idea!" Zoe snapped, her bravado wilting. "Quick, let's try that way." She walked briskly to the end of the corridor, turned and walked along another passage. Then another. And another. All identical, and all leading nowhere. She gulped. "It's a labyrinth. Hera's trapped us in a maze! We could be stuck for hours. Days, even."

Tim's breath caught in his throat. "Can't we climb over?" He placed a hand against the wall. It was made of slippery polished marble and he couldn't get a grip. "Climb on my back and try to get across."

Tim got onto his hands and knees and Zoe stood on his back. Her sandals dug sharply into his spine as she reached up. Tim gritted his teeth and tried not to moan.

"It's too high," Zoe said, grunting with the effort. She slithered back down. "Dad'll go nuts when he knows I'm missing!"

"Don't worry, we'll find a way out." Tim straightened up, sounding more certain than he felt. He rubbed at his back.

"That's the spirit," a smooth voice said.

"Never give up!"

Tim snapped his head around. A young man with floppy blond hair was leaning lazily against a wall. "Wha– Who are you?"

"Theseus."

The young man pushed himself off the wall. He glanced at his reflection in the shiny marble, smiled, then sauntered toward them.

Tim heard Zoe take a sharp breath. The name was familiar to him, but he couldn't place it. He looked at Zoe, and was surprised to find her eyes soft with adoration.

"Yep," Theseus said with a swagger. "Son of Aegeus, King of Athens. I'm the Minotaur Slayer, the greatest hero in all of Greece. At your service." He flicked a salute at them. Zoe's face turned pink.

"I know who you are!" Hope surged through Tim. "You fought that bull monster. It lived in a maze, right? You killed it and rescued the kids trapped there."

Theseus winked. "That's me. Want my autograph? Maybe later, kid. Anyway, I heard on the GGG that you needed help, so here I am. Ready to be a hero again!"

"GGG?"

"Greek God Grapevine," Zoe whispered, her eyes never leaving Theseus' face. "Gods use it to pass messages to heroes. You know, warnings, instructions. Things like that."

Tim screwed his face up, trying to picture it. There were no computers in Ancient Greece. Not even phones. "So is it, like, a real grapevine?"

"Well, what else would it be? The god talks into a tendril and the message goes through all the leaves. The grapes change color, too. Red for danger, green for glory."

Tim thought it sounded marvelous. "Can anyone use it?" He wouldn't mind having a go.

"No, just gods and heroes. Like Theseus."

Zoe's voice trembled slightly as she said his name. "How did you find us so quickly, Theseus?"

"As soon as I entered the maze, my amazing powers erupted like a fountain and guided me to you." The hero struck a gallant pose. "It wasn't just luck or anything like that."

"Wow." Zoe looked impressed. "And how are you going to rescue us?"

"With a ball of string! I place one end at the entrance, unwind it as I go, then follow it back out. Simple!"

"Cool." Tim looked around, but he couldn't see the piece of string marking out the trail. "Where is it?"

"Oh. Yes. Sadly I was in such a rush to

be awesome, I forgot to bring it. Never mind," the hero said perkily, "I'll find something else. Oh, this'll do."

Theseus snatched Tim's hand-knitted scarf and started to unravel it.

"HEY! DON'T DO THAT!"

"We need string."

"But it won't help. It's too late now." Theseus looked blank and Tim hastened to explain. "It only works if you put it at the entrance *before* you enter the labyrinth."

"If you say so." Shrugging, Theseus draped the straggly scarf back over Tim's shoulders. "Don't say I didn't try."

"Theseus, isn't there something you can do?" Zoe's eyes shone beseechingly.

"I'm sure … I think … ah, yes." Theseus rummaged around in a leather pouch that hung off his belt. After a few moments, he pulled out a small round hand mirror. The handsome hero shook out his hair and pouted at his reflection.

"How does that help?" Tim asked
impatiently.

"Hey, we may be trapped, but at least my
good looks can cheer us all up."

Zoe nodded and grinned and admired
the hero's reflection.

Tim sighed.

He sank to the floor, hope fading fast.

Tim sat on the cold hard ground and stared at the soaring marble walls. He looked from the star-struck Zoe to their would-be rescuer Theseus, and realized it was up to him to find a solution. But how? How could they escape from the labyrinth that Hera had trapped them in? They'd already spent the better part of an hour wandering up and down identical-looking corridors and trying unsuccessfully to scramble over the slippery walls. He needed to think of something smarter.

"Theseus, tell us again how you rescued the young Athenians." Zoe knelt on the ground next to the hero, her eyes shining.

"Of course." Theseus made himself comfortable before continuing. "You see, it all started when I discovered that human tributes were being sent to Crete to be eaten by the Minotaur. Being such an awesome hero, I decided to …"

Theseus droned on and on, making it hard for Tim to concentrate. He wished he had earplugs to block out the boasting. Turning his back on them, he focused on letting his mind wander free. Up and down the corridors, trying to picture what the maze might look like from above. As if it were a computer game …

… a computer game like …

Like *Maze of Miracles*, his favorite when he was little! Tim always used to get stuck on Level 3, until he finally made a breakthrough. Follow an unbroken line and keep going left. It worked in the game. Might it also work in real life? It was worth a try.

"And so the beautiful Ariadne, who naturally fell madly in love with me–"

"I think I know how to get out." Tim interrupted the hero.

Theseus clicked his tongue in irritation. "Can't it wait? I'm up to the bit where–"

"No, it can't. Come on, Zoe." Tim pulled

the girl to her feet. "Follow me."

Ignoring Theseus' grumbling, Tim placed his left hand against a wall. "All we have to do is keep one hand on the wall as we walk. Don't take it off." He marched gamely on ahead, with the fingers on his free hand crossed.

Before too long the unrelenting whiteness of the marble walls was punctured by a rectangle of jumbled color. It had to be the exit! Tim ran down the corridor, his feet gliding on the slippery tiles. He burst outside, then skidded to a halt.

Tim groaned. "No. I don't believe it!"

"WHAT'S WRONG?"

Zoe asked, hot on his heels. "Are we still trapped? We can't be."

"Flowers." Tim gazed out at the rows and rows of blossoms stretching out into the distance. "Nothing but blooming flowers."

After having spent all morning at a garden center, Tim couldn't bear the thought of more blossoms. But at least it was warm and sunny here, not cold and drizzly like it was at home. And Leo the bully certainly wasn't about to make a surprise appearance.

"Do you recognize this place?" Tim looked at Zoe and Theseus. "Think you can find the way home?"

Zoe bit her lip and shook her head. "No,

but we have to hurry. We've got to get that vase before Hera can use it to trap my dad, if she hasn't already!"

Theseus, looking bored, wandered off to one side. Tim's stomach let out another mighty rumble and he grinned sheepishly. He looked at a row of sunflowers and remembered what he'd seen at the garden center.

"Any idea how to get the seeds out?" he asked Zoe. "I haven't had lunch. Don't worry," he added when she flashed him an impatient look. "I can eat as we walk."

"Here," she said, pushing in front of him. She squeezed out a double handful and thrust them at Tim. "We've got to keep moving. Let's follow Theseus – he'll get us home."

Tim doubted it. He crammed the seeds in his jeans pocket and was surprised to find that the crushed sunflower from the garden center was still there. He started nibbling at the seeds, wishing he were nibbling on a roast chicken instead.

Theseus sauntered over to a section of the garden filled with life-sized statues. Hands linked behind his back, he peered into their faces like a general inspecting his soldiers. "This one's ugly," he muttered. "So's this one. And this."

"They're not as good looking as you," Zoe simpered, her need for haste momentarily forgotten.

"That goes without saying," the hero said, flicking back his floppy bangs.

Tim glanced at the statues and was surprised to find that Theseus was right. They *were* somewhat ugly. Or rather, they weren't as attractive as would be expected. Most of the Greek statues he'd seen before had strong, relaxed bodies and flawless features; these had warts and wrinkles and scars. Some were hunched over in fear; others looked like they were trying to flee. Some had their hands thrust up in the air as if trying to ward off danger. All of the statues had

looks of horror on their faces, as if they had witnessed something dreadful. Who on earth would want to put something like that in their garden?

Curious, Tim stepped closer to one of the smaller statues. It was a boy about his size. And it was crying!

How could that be?

Tim put his finger on the boy's cheek to check. It came away wet. He glanced at the cloudless sky. It couldn't be rain. Tim walked along a row of statues and saw that several others also appeared to be crying.

"Zoe, come look. You're not going to believe this but—"

The sound of footsteps interrupted him, followed by a loud hiss. It sounded like a dozen angry snakes, all spitting in unison.

Zoe froze. "What was that?"

"I don't know," Tim replied. "But it's getting closer."

7

The footsteps grew louder. Someone – or something – was walking steadily toward them; the sound of hissing snakes grew more frenzied with each step.

From the corner of his eye, Tim caught a glimpse of a tall, thin woman weaving her way toward them through the rows of flowers. Was it Hera? Had she found them? He snapped his head around for a better look. The woman

appeared to be searching for something.
Tim couldn't see her face, but he could
tell it wasn't the goddess. Hera had
been wearing a regal ivory-colored
gown with a gossamer veil
trailing down her back.
This woman's dress was
dull and black. Tattered
and loose, it hung off her
body like rags.

He should have felt
relieved, but

something about the woman's appearance sent a shiver down Tim's spine. Then he realized what it was.

Her hair. Brownish-green and stripy, the thick clumps curled and twisted about as if they were alive.

"Zoe? Someone's coming toward us. I know it sounds crazy, but I think she's got snakes for hair."

"What?" Zoe jumped. "Don't look at her! Tim, Theseus, turn away!"

The Minotaur Slayer immediately slapped his hands over his eyes and stood motionless. He looked like one of those little kids that thought that if they couldn't see you, you couldn't see them.

"How come?" Tim tried to get a better

look at the woman but Zoe pinched his arm. Hard.

"Ow. Stop that."

"NO! LISTEN TO ME. DO. NOT. LOOK."

Turning his back on the mysterious woman, Tim glared at Zoe, who had also positioned herself so she couldn't see. He folded his arms across his chest. "Happy? Now she can sneak up on us and we won't even know."

"We need to walk away. Start moving forward."

"What about him?' Tim jerked his thumb at Theseus, whose hands were still firmly clamped over his eyes. Blushing furiously, Zoe grasped the hero's elbow and steered him around a cluster of agonized-looking statues. Tim followed. "Is anyone going to explain what's going on?"

"Keep moving," Zoe said, her voice shaky. "She's a gorgon. One look at her face and you turn to stone."

Tim nearly tripped over his own feet as the realization hit him.

"Does that mean? Oh no, the statues!" That was why they looked so lifelike. They weren't statues at all, not really. They were ordinary people who'd been turned to stone as they tried to escape. He peered into the horrified face of the frozen figure in front of him and waved his hand in front of its eyes. "Can't we help them?"

"Not now. We have to hide. If she can't see us, she might go away."

"Do you think she's looking for us?" Tim asked, his heart hammering in his chest.

Zoe shrugged. "Who knows? We can't go up and ask her. Maybe she doesn't know we're here – but we can't take that chance."

Tim looked along the endless rows of flowers. How could they hide behind a daisy? Unless the gorgon was blind, she'd easily spot them. "Theseus, can you find us a good place to hide?" Tim thought it was about time the hero started acting like one.

Theseus' fingers parted just enough for him to peep at Tim. "Nope. Can't see a thing. Sorry." And he shut his eyes again.

Tim was about to protest when Zoe took a sharp breath.

"THERE. WHAT'S THAT?"

He followed her gaze. One edge of the garden was bordered by a soaring cliff with scraggly bushes at its base. Its crumpled face was speckled with sunlight and shadow. Tim didn't understand. "How does that help? It's a dead end. We'll be trapped."

"Look there." She jabbed the air with her finger.

At first Tim didn't see it, but then a broad grin crossed his face.

■　■　■

The coolness of the cave welcomed them, hiding them from view. Blinking, Tim waited for his eyes to adjust to the dim light. "All right, Theseus, you can look now."

"Is it safe?" the hero whispered, coming to a halt.

"I hope so. We found a cave. With a bit

of luck that gorgon thing didn't see us come in."

Theseus peered through his fingers. He squinted at the stalactite-dotted ceiling and narrow cave opening. He must have felt reassured because he dropped his hands to his sides and squared his shoulders. "Lucky you kids were with me." The hero flicked back his bangs and smiled down at Zoe, who was looking all gooey again. "I said I'd keep you safe, didn't I?"

"You did, yes. You're the greatest hero in all of Greece."

"WHAT?"

Tim squawked. How could she still think that? He was about to speak his mind, then realized there was no point. Not while Zoe had that silly look in her eyes. "Tell me more about this gorgon," he said instead, moving farther into the cave. Although it was narrow, it seemed quite deep. Several openings trailed off between the towering stalagmites that reached up toward the ceiling.

"There were three originally." Zoe reluctantly tore her gaze away from the hero. "But now there are only two left. Dad talks about them a lot because his great-grandfather was the only person ever to kill a gorgon. Her name was Medusa."

That gave Tim hope. "Great! Did your dad tell you how he did it?"

"Ye-e-s. Yes, he did." Zoe lapsed into silence.

A heartbeat passed. "So what did he do? Come on, Zoe, this is important!"

Zoe wouldn't meet Tim's eye. He clicked his tongue impatiently and she finally replied. "Well, how would I know? I wasn't listening."

"Oh great," Tim muttered, kicking a pebble with his shoe. "So now what are we meant to do? Sit and wait for the gorgon to find us? In case you haven't noticed, we're trapped. There's nowhere to go. We don't know how to fight her. If she comes into the cave, we've had it."

"If you keep your voice down," Zoe said hotly, not keeping her voice down in the slightest, "she might give up and go away. But if you keep whining, she'll know where we are."

"Children, children, don't bicker," Theseus said, raising his hands in a grand gesture. "I'm here. I'll protect you."

Tim didn't feel any better but he kept his thoughts to himself. It was hard to believe that Theseus was actually the famous Minotaur Slayer. Maybe he'd only defeated the bull-headed beast by accident. By boasting so much he bored it to death, perhaps. Could Theseus stop a gorgon, whose glance turned people to stone? Tim doubted it. All he could hope for was that Hercules, worried about his daughter, would somehow find them and rescue them. His great-grandfather had killed a gorgon: surely he would know what to do.

A rustling sound made Tim jump.

The gorgon! Had she found them?

The noise seemed to be
coming from behind them,
from deeper inside the
cave. Could she have
crept up on them
through another
entrance?

Before Tim could
warn the others,
a figure hobbled
out from
behind a thick
limestone
column.

Leaning heavily on a walking stick, the old man was as gnarled and wizened as the column itself. His eyebrows shot to the top of his wrinkled head when he saw them, and at first it looked like he was about to start yelling. Then he looked more carefully at Zoe and a smile lit up his face.

"Is that my great-great-granddaughter, who never comes to visit me?"

"Grandpa! Yes, it's me." Zoe ran over and hugged him. "I didn't know you lived here."

The old man sniffed. "I've lived in this cave since before you were born. Well, you're here now. How is that muscle-headed father of yours? He didn't come with you? Always too busy, that's his problem. No time to appreciate my begonias. They're particularly fine this year, don't you think?"

Tim wished Zoe's relative would keep his voice down. He was talking so loudly, the gorgon was sure to hear them.

"He's well," Zoe said. "I hope. Um, Grandpa …"

The old man turned his watery gaze on Tim and Theseus. "I see you've brought friends. Introduce them, child."

Zoe obeyed and Tim saw the old man's eyes narrow as he looked Theseus up and down. "Killed the Minotaur, eh? Piece of cake. I slew the dreaded Medusa when your grandfather was in diapers."

Relief flooded through Tim as he

made the connection. "Ah! So you're–"

"Perseus, at your service," the old man said, bowing so low his bones creaked. "Once the greatest hero in all of Greece. Mind you, I haven't done anything heroic lately. Unless you count battling freesia fungus and rose rot!" His chuckle turned into a wheeze and he had to pause for breath. "But I've always kept myself ready to fight. See, I've even made my retirement home in a gorgon's garden, on hand to be a hero again if required."

Tim couldn't help thinking of all the poor people turned to stone and how they had needed a hero.

Theseus seemed to be thinking along the same lines. "And yet you haven't slain the gorgon?" he said, arms folded across his chest. "Doesn't sound too heroic to me."

"WHY WOULD I?"

Perseus snapped. "She doesn't bother me. In fact, she rather likes me looking after her garden. It's never looked finer. Have you seen my gladiolas, young man? Think you could do better?"

Tim felt he should interrupt before the argument between the two heroes turned into a fist fight. "Can you tell us how you did it? How you killed Medusa, I mean? This other gorgon's after us."

"Of course. Her name is Stheno, by the way. The first one's sister. She wasn't too

happy when I killed Medusa, I can tell you."
The old man eased himself onto a
stalagmite that was conveniently stool-
shaped, and motioned for them to gather
round. "I did something very clever. I
used my shiny metal shield to look at her
reflection. I didn't look at her directly,
understand?"

Tim nodded.

"That kept me safe. And then – *whack!*
– I lopped her snaky head off with
my sword." Perseus made a slashing
motion with his arm, the wasted muscles
sagging. "One ex-gorgon! That head kept
its power, mind you. Even chopped off, it
could still turn people to stone." The old
man smiled as if relishing the memory.

That was all well and good, Tim thought, but could that help them now? They didn't have a shiny shield, let alone a sword.

As if reading his thoughts, Perseus interrupted them. "I've still got that shield, if you'd care to see it. Zoe, go into the back there and fetch it."

"Just in time, by the sound of it," Theseus said as Zoe scampered off.

Tim didn't need to strain to hear the hissing snakes. The gorgon sounded very close.

Zoe returned, lugging a large round shield. "Is this it? It's all rusty." As she spoke, a giant flake of rust fell off the pockmarked surface. It looked as if one

solid kick would make the whole thing disintegrate.

"Needs a bit of a polish, that's all."

Tim tugged experimentally at the shield and a chunk of it came away in his hand.

"It was a long time ago." Perseus sighed. "At least the shield lasted longer than my sword. That rusted away decades ago."

Tim groaned. "Now what do we do? She's getting nearer!"

Perseus stroked the few straggly gray hairs that passed for his beard. "We could try pelting her with flowers. I picked some lovely pink roses this morning. They've got very sharp thorns. I reckon they could do some serious damage."

Tim didn't have time to reply. Before he could speak, the gorgon entered the cave.

9

"Look away!" Zoe shouted. "She's here."

Tim could hear the angry hiss of the gorgon's hair-snakes as she entered the cave. He, Zoe and the others spun to face the wall. It was awful knowing that the monster was feet away, and that simply looking at her face would turn them to stone. Tim kept his eyes clamped tightly shut and hoped that his friends would do the same.

"What do we do? We can't stay here forever! We've got to get that vase before Hera can use it." Zoe sounded more angry than frightened.

Tim reached out and groped around for her hand. Soft and trembling, he squeezed it tight. "It'll be okay. Don't worry, I'm sure your dad's fine. By now he'll know you're missing and he'll come and find us."

"My father? King Aegeus? He died years ago – I don't think he can help."

"Urgh."

Tim dropped Theseus' hand like it was a hot potato. That was the problem with doing things blind. He nearly made the mistake of opening his eyes, but remembered not to just in time. "I meant Zoe's dad. Hercules. He'll save us."

"I very much doubt that," came Perseus' feeble voice. "He'd try to catch Stheno's eye so she could admire the muscles on his muscles … No. We are on our own."

"As long as we don't look at her, she can't hurt us. We'll wait it out," Tim said, shifting his weight in an attempt to get more comfortable. "She can't force us to look at her."

"It's not as simple as that." There was a grim respect in Perseus' voice. "Gorgons are very clever. They can find a way to trick you into looking. They never get tired. And they never give up."

Tim shivered. He couldn't imagine what sort of trick could make him open his eyes. He vowed to keep them shut, no matter what.

"ARGH, HELP!"

Zoe's voice shrieked loudly in his left ear. "Stheno's got my arm! She's pulling me! She's dragging me away. Help, Tim!"

Tim whirled around in the direction of the voice. Thrusting out his hands, he grabbed onto some fabric. "I've got you! Hold on, Zoe."

A loud tearing sound filled the air.

Tim's hands came away and his eyes snapped open. He'd ripped Zoe's clothes! Except … the piece of material hanging in his hands was black, nothing like Zoe's bright-red chiton. Black and bedraggled, it smelled like rotting flesh. Disgusted, he dropped the crumbling cloth and wiped his hands on his jeans.

"No!" Zoe's voice now came from the opposite direction. "That wasn't me. It was

Stheno copying my voice. Don't listen to her."

Tim realized how easily he'd been tricked after all. The only thing that had saved him was the fact that the gorgon hadn't been facing him directly when he'd opened his eyes.

Tim felt a tickle of breath on his face. Unlike the warmth of human breath, this was icy cold. It smelled of dust and mildew, like old books stored in a damp basement. The gorgon must be standing right in front of him, peering into his face. He froze. All it would take was one tiny flicker of his eyelid …

"There must be something we can do," he heard Zoe say. He thought it was the real Zoe this time, as the voice was some way off to his right. "Any ideas, anyone?"

Tim was finding it very hard to concentrate. He turned toward Zoe and shuffled forward, trying to get some distance between himself and Stheno.

"If only we had a decent weapon, I'd soon show the gorgon what's what," Theseus said with relish. "But as everything here is old and useless …"

"I know what you're implying, young man," Perseus said, thumping his walking stick on the ground. "Don't think I'm too old to understand. Just because I prefer gardening to chasing after monsters–"

"Hang on." An idea occurred to Tim. His words tumbled over each other in excitement. "What about your gardening tools? Perseus, isn't there something we could use? A shovel or a rake or something?"

"There's my scythe," the aged hero said after a pause. "Best quality. Forged by Hephaestus himself, the god of blacksmiths. Given to me as a reward for my prize dahlias. Beautiful they were, all firm and glossy." He sighed. "I use the scythe to trim the lawn and it gives a lovely straight edge. I don't want it damaged, mind."

"That sounds ideal. Can you get it? Can you give it to Theseus?"

A series of groans and shuffling footsteps followed as Perseus edged his way down the narrow cave. Then there was an exclamation of satisfaction. "Take it," Tim heard Perseus say. "Don't wreck it."

Tim heard Theseus grunt as he picked up the large cutting blade. "Righto," said the hero. The scythe whooshed through the air as Theseus tested it out. "Good balance. Strong and sharp. This'll do nicely. Let me at her."

"NOT YET!

You still can't open your eyes." Tim rubbed his forehead. If only they had something like the reflective shield that Perseus had once used to slay Medusa. "Do you have anything flat and shiny? Something we can use to look at her reflection?"

"Sorry, son, not a thing," Perseus replied.

"No problem. I can use my super-senses and find her anyway." Theseus chuckled as he slashed with the scythe. "Who needs eyesight? I can be a hero blindfolded!"

Tim heard the blade slicing through the dank cave air. He stepped back as he felt it whizz mere inches past his nose. "No you can't! It's too risky. You could hit one of us."

"Fussy, fussy," Theseus grunted, the scythe thumping as he rested it on the floor. "So now what?"

"Maybe we should try to get out of the cave, then make a run for it. Zoe, grab my shirt and we'll leave."

Tim waited until he felt Zoe's tug. Hands groping outward, he took a few small, experimental steps forward. He swung his head around, seeking the sunlight that flooded in through the cave's entrance. It was so bright he could see the rosy glow though

his closed eyelids. If they kept walking forward …

The floor of the narrow cave was uneven and Tim stumbled, falling to his knees. Zoe tripped and slammed into him, sending them both sprawling. "Oof!"

"Ouch. Sorry."

"Here, take my hand." Theseus' voice came from directly in front of Tim.

Glad that the vain hero was being useful for once, Tim reached out. However, the hand that grasped his was neither soft nor trembling. It was as hard and cold as marble. It didn't belong to Theseus.

It wasn't even human.

Using all his willpower, Tim fought his instinct to open his eyes. He gritted his teeth and wrenched his hand away from the gorgon's icy grasp. He rubbed his hand on his pants, trying to bring some warmth back into his chilled fingers. That was way too close for comfort. From now on, he vowed silently, he would trust no one. Stheno's ability to imitate his friends' voices was just too good.

"Tim?" Zoe sounded uncertain. "Was that Theseus? Or was that *her*?"

Tim didn't answer. That could be Stheno trying to trick him again. He felt someone grasp his shoulder and his whole body jolted.

"Relax, it's me." A warm, girl-sized hand brushed his cheek. "See?"

"Okay, I believe you. But keep your voice down." Tim leaned toward what he hoped was his friend. "We don't want her to know everything we're saying. We don't want her to hear our plan."

"That's true." Zoe sounded encouraged. "Does that mean you've got one?"

"Um, not yet."

"Oh. Great." She clicked her tongue.

"I'll just have to think of something myself."

Time stretched out as Tim and his friends sat in darkness and silence. Eventually a soft snoring started up, echoing off the sloping walls. Tim thought it was probably Perseus dozing. The sound was oddly comforting. Better by far than the other noises he could hear: those of the gorgon moving around the cave, her dress rustling and her hair-snakes hissing.

There had to be something they could do. They had the weapon. They had the hero. All they needed was a way to look at Stheno without looking at her. If only Perseus' shield hadn't rusted …

"You know what's a shame?" Theseus'

voice drifted across the cave. Tim nudged Zoe to keep quiet. He didn't want them to say anything until they were sure it was the hero speaking and not the gorgon. "It's a shame we have to keep our eyes shut. Otherwise, we could all be cheered up by the sight of my handsome face."

Tim exhaled. That was Theseus, all right.

"You remember," the hero continued. "Like in Hera's labyrinth. And that worked out well, didn't it? There's nothing better for keeping our spirits high than a glimpse of sheer perfection."

"You're so right …" Zoe's voice trailed off, and Tim felt her suddenly go rigid next to him. "That's it!" she squealed. "Of course!"

"WHAT?"

"Theseus." Zoe spoke urgently. "In the maze. Get it?"

Tim face-palmed himself for not thinking of it before. How could he have forgotten the hero's display of vanity in Hera's labyrinth? But there was another problem. Tim had to explain their idea to Theseus without Stheno overhearing, in case she found a way to thwart it.

"Actually," Tim said loudly, "It might be enough simply to touch your handsome face." It was hard for him to say that without laughing, but he did his best.

"You think so? All right. Come toward the sound of my voice."

Tim felt Zoe start to rise next to him and he pressed down on her shoulder, making it clear she wasn't to follow. Thankfully she had the sense not to protest. He shuffled toward the hero gingerly, testing each step before moving. He did not want to fall again. The short walk seemed to take forever.

"That's it – you're here." Theseus' voice was directly in front of Tim. "You may touch my face. Gently now, I don't want you to leave any marks."

Tim risked opening his eyes briefly. Rather than reaching up to touch the hero, however, he made a grab for the leather satchel that Theseus wore strung around his waist.

"Hey! What do you think you're doing? That's mine." Theseus clamped his hand protectively over the satchel.

"Your mirror," Tim hissed. "Use it." He resisted the urge to glance over his shoulder.

"Oh yes, good idea." Dropping the scythe, Theseus pulled the small round hand mirror out of its pouch. "Now I can be cheered up too." He pouted at his reflection before shaking

out his hair and striking a heroic pose.

"NOT LIKE THAT!"

Tim yelped. "To fight the gorgon. Quick, before she sees us."

But it was too late. A loud screeching reverberated through the air as Stheno rushed toward them.

Tim snatched the mirror from Theseus. "Use it to look at her! But first grab the scythe, so you're ready."

"Oh, I see! Got it." Theseus had finally caught on to the idea. He hoisted the heavy cutting blade, which glimmered faintly in the dim light. "Where is she? Is she behind me? I can't hear the snakes anymore."

It was true. After Stheno's loud screech faded into silence, her hair-snakes had stopped their sibilant hissing. Tim didn't think that was a good sign. It could mean that they were about to strike. A sense of urgency pulsed through him. "I'll angle the mirror." With a shaking hand, he held it up high. "Is that right? Can you see her?"

"No. Twist it a bit that way," the hero said, shifting his head and jerking his thumb. Tim adjusted the angle. "Better?" He tried various options but

the hero kept shaking his head.

"It's like she's vanished off the face of the earth. Do you think she's gone?"

Tim didn't think so. He thought it more likely that the gorgon was trying a new trick – hiding so that they would either look for her or think she had left – before revealing herself. He strained his ears for the slightest sound. The hissing had stopped, but he thought he could hear something else. A whisper-quiet flapping that barely disturbed the air. "Perseus," he said, his voice low. "Are there bats in your cave?"

A gentle snore told him that Perseus wasn't going to be very helpful.

"It doesn't sound like bats," Theseus

whispered. "Do you think it might be–"

Theseus' sentence was cut off by another loud screech as the gorgon swooped down on them. She'd been flying! Possibly even hovering above their heads the whole time. Theseus slashed with the scythe but missed.

"What's happening?" Zoe demanded.

"Don't look!" Tim said. "Try again," he urged the hero.

"Duck!" Theseus called, slashing away as Stheno swooped again.

Tim threw himself face down onto the ground and felt a powerful gust of air as the gorgon beat her wings over his head. He scuttled backward as Theseus blindly thrust the blade toward him. Judging by

the grunted oath, the hero had missed
again.

"THE MIRROR."

The gust had blown it out of Tim's hand.
Any hope he had was starting to crumble.
Stheno always seemed to be one step ahead
of them. Tim couldn't risk looking for the
mirror in case he caught a glimpse of her
face. He shut his eyes and groped about on
the floor blindly. Something hard bumped
against his hand and he grabbed it.

"Let go of my foot," Theseus snapped.

"What are you doing?"

Tim didn't answer as his hand closed around a familiar object. He opened his eyes and held the mirror up in triumph. Now they could fight her safely! But when he saw the reflection glaring back at him, he screamed and almost dropped the mirror again.

Stheno was standing directly behind him. She was more hideous than he could have possibly imagined. Sunken cheeks, with skin the color of a dead fish. Her eyes were a dirty yellow and her pupils were elongated slits, like those of the snakes that twisted and writhed grotesquely around her face. The gorgon's shriveled black lips parted over needle-like teeth as another inhuman screech erupted from her throat. Her wings looked nothing like the majestic angels' wings that Tim had seen on television. They were dirty, gray, moldy things, folded tight against her body.

"THESEUS! SHE'S HERE. LOOK!"

Trying to stop himself from trembling, Tim thrust the mirror up and around so that Theseus could see Stheno.

Without hesitation, the hero twisted his torso and swung the scythe with such force that the air molecules around it rang

like a bell. The gorgon screeched and tried
to fly out of his reach but the roof of
the cave was too low. Her wings tangled
around a cluster of jutting stalactites and
she roared with rage as she tried to pull
herself free. The stalactites creaked from
the pressure but held firm.

Tim winced as a loud *SNICK*
reverberated through the cave,
followed by a hollow thud as the
gorgon's decapitated head fell to
the ground. A bright flash of light lit up
the cave as if a hundred fireworks had
been set off. Tim looked away, grateful his
stomach was empty.

"Yes!" Theseus pumped his fist in triumph.
"I am the greatest! The bravest, strongest,

cleverest and best-looking hero in all of
Greece!" He struck a pose and grinned.

Zoe jumped to her feet, a look of joy
lighting up her face. "You did it! I knew you
would. Oh, Theseus, you saved us." She ran
over and threw her arms around the hero.

"The clothes, watch the clothes,"
Theseus murmured, brushing himself
off. "They're dusty enough as it is, thanks
to this festering cave." He pointed to a
wooden stool near his feet. "You may
admire me from down there."

Zoe sat obediently, her eyes shining. "Isn't he marvelous, Grandpa?"

There was no reply.

"Grandpa?"

Perseus wasn't responding. Tim and Zoe exchanged a glance and walked toward the old man, who was sitting hunched over on a chair. He hadn't made any noise for a while now, Tim realized. Even the snoring had stopped. Tim checked him over for signs of life, but Perseus was utterly still.

As still as a statue, in fact.

"Oh no, Grandpa! Are you all right?" Zoe rushed to the old man, nearly bowling him over. "Did you look at the gorgon's face? You told us not to!"

With a loud, barking snore, Perseus snapped awake. "What? What's happening?" He blinked in alarm at the girl clinging to him. "Zoe, what's wrong?"

Heaving a sigh of relief, Zoe pulled away. "Grandpa, we thought the gorgon turned you to stone. You weren't speaking, you weren't moving. You looked …"

"Just taking an unexpected nap, my dear," Perseus said, patting his great-great-

granddaughter's head awkwardly. "That happens at my age, I'm afraid." The aged hero looked blearily at Tim and Theseus. "What happened to Stheno? Did she leave?"

Talking over each other in their eagerness to tell the story, they explained how Theseus had decapitated the monster while Tim held the mirror up for him.

Perseus cackled with delight. "Good trick that, if I do say so myself." He rubbed his hands together. "Now, what did you do with her head? Put it away safely, did you? I don't want it harming my hydrangeas. I've had enough trouble with root rot."

"It's where it fell. Over there."

Tim started to turn in Stheno's direction.

"AH, NO!"

Perseus jerked forward, his joints creaking. "Even though the gorgon's dead, her head's as dangerous as ever. Looking at her face will still turn you to stone."

Feeling the blood drain out of his cheeks, Tim twisted back around.

"That's what happened to Polydectes, a brutish king who kept pestering my mother." Perseus' face broke into a crinkled grin. "The king was the one who'd ordered me to kill Medusa. To be honest, I think he was just trying to get rid of me. Anyway, I placed the head in a satchel and took it back to him. Polydectes didn't believe I'd killed her and he insisted on taking a look. The head turned him stone dead."

"What did you do with the head, Grandpa?" Zoe asked. "Afterward, I mean."

"I gave it to the goddess Athena. She

put it on her shield. I don't think there's enough room on it for another gorgon head, though."

"Just shove it in a box," Theseus said, releasing a crick in his neck. "I should get going. My fans will be missing me, and it's not fair to deprive them of my presence any longer. They're going to want to hear all about my latest heroic feat."

"Children, fetch that casket." Perseus pointed at an ornately carved box that lay tucked in a nook in the cave wall. The size of a small suitcase, the casket was made of polished dark wood. The carvings depicted battle scenes and Tim thought one of the figures might be Hercules.

"I had been using it to store tulip bulbs, but it's empty now. You can use it for the head."

Tim and Zoe grasped a handle each and lifted the casket. Tim shook it slightly to make sure it really was empty. He didn't want to open it and find another gorgon head inside.

"I'll get the head," he said.

"Hang on." Zoe pulled Tim's frayed scarf off from around his shoulders and used it to fashion a makeshift blindfold. "Can't be too careful."

Nodding his thanks, Tim got down onto his hands and knees and started groping his way across the floor, heading in the direction where the gorgon had fallen.

Pieces of grit pricked at his palms but he kept going. Eventually his hand rested on something cold and squishy and he let out an involuntary yelp. "I – I think I've got it!" Trying not to think about what he was doing, he grabbed a fistful of dead snake-hair and pulled. The gorgon's head was heavier than he'd expected and it thudded across the floor.

The others closed their eyes and called out encouragingly so that Tim could follow the direction of

their voices. Finally, panting, he bumped into the casket and hoisted the head up and in. A deep *thunk* echoed throughout the cave and Tim slammed down the lid. Only then did he take off his blindfold. Draping the scarf back around his shoulders, he said, "You can look now. All safe."

"Yay! Well done." Zoe clapped and smiled at him, but her eyes didn't shine with hero worship the way they did when she looked at Theseus. Tim discovered that he was rather relieved.

"Now what do we do with it?" Zoe asked. "We can't waste any more time here; we need to get that vase."

"Leave the casket with me," Perseus said. "Hardly anybody comes to visit these days.

No one will even know it's here. You go on home and give my regards to your lovely mother. As for your father, tell him he's lucky to have such a dutiful child."

Zoe gave the old man a hug. "Don't forget the head's there, and try to store bulbs in it again."

Chuckling, Perseus ruffled his great-great-granddaughter's hair. "Don't you worry about that. Do you know how to get back?" He described the route home, then fixed his watery gaze on Theseus. "I assume you'll accompany the children? They need to be protected against any further dangers."

"Yes yes, of course, let's go." The hero was walking away as he spoke and Zoe scuttled after him. Tim waved at the old man and followed. The sun was bright after the darkness of the cave, making him shade his eyes and squint. He looked away from the unfortunate statues, saddened by the thought that there was nothing he could do to help them. Zoe skipped along the path as she gazed up at Theseus.

Tim wished he could share her happiness. Naturally he was relieved to have escaped Hera's labyrinth and the gorgon, but he knew his problems weren't over yet. He was stuck in Ancient Greece, far from home. His mother had no idea where he was and was sure to be worrying about him. As far as she knew, he had simply vanished. All Zoe had to do was follow the path and then she would be home with her parents. But how was he going to make his way back to England? And how could he jump forward in time thousands of years? Tim suspected his problems were only just beginning.

13

"Hey, is that Theseus? It is! Oh wow. Theseus, over here! Hi!" A group of teenage girls giggled and waved when the hero looked their way.

Having escaped the gorgon, the three were on their way back to Zoe's house. They crossed a stretch of exposed countryside before reaching the familiar village. Tim, Zoe and Theseus had only been walking for a little while when they were waylaid by a bunch of fangirls.

"It sure is, girls. Hi right back at ya!"

Theseus winked as he pointed his fingers at the simpering group clustered around a well.

"Have you saved any lives today, Theseus?" a tall blonde girl called out.

Zoe glowered at the girl but the hero didn't seem to notice. "Sure did," he said, and was met with a chorus of cheers. "These cute little fellas right here. Wanna hear about it?" With a toss of his head, he flicked his long floppy bangs off his forehead and grinned.

"You're supposed to be seeing us home," Tim pointed out.

"Later, kid, later." Theseus sauntered

off toward the girls, leaving Zoe staring wistfully after him. The hero started talking before he even reached the well.

"You see it all started when I learned on the GGG that some kids were trapped in Hera's labyrinth. As you know, I'm something of an expert on labyrinths and so …"

"COME ON, LET'S GO."

Tim pulled Zoe by the arm.

She shook him off. "Shouldn't we wait?"

"For him? Forget it. He'll be hours."

"But he's meant to stay with me."

Tim glanced at the sun, which was hanging low in the sky. "If we don't leave now, it'll be nearly dark by the time you're home. Your dad will go nuts."

"If he's still there." As Zoe dragged her gaze away from her idol, her voice took on a note of anxiety. "Maybe Hera

managed to catch him after all."

"I'm sure your dad will be fine." Tim repeated his reassurances. "Like I said, he's not going to walk straight into another trap."

Zoe flashed Tim an impatient look. "Then you don't know my dad very well. Come on, let's go back to Hera's temple and get the vase."

"Now? Can't we try again later?"

Zoe shook her head. "Dad's sure to punish me for leaving the house without permission. He might not let me out again for ages. No, we have to do it now or we might never get the chance. Come on, it's this way."

Not knowing how to stop the

determined girl, Tim let Zoe lead the way.

By the time they reached Hera's temple, the first flush of sunset had started. Soft golden streaks crossed the sky. Tim still hadn't worked out how he might return to his own time. But first things first: he had to recover the vase, see Zoe safely home, face Hercules' questions about why they had left the house and why they were gone for so long. Only after all that could he think about how he would get back. He tried to push the troubling thoughts of his worried mother out of his mind, but they kept resurfacing. Images of her searching the streets for him flashed before his eyes.

"There's no one here," Zoe said and the image dissolved again. "Come on, quick."

The children dashed up the temple stairs, eyes darting left and right as they checked that Hera wasn't lurking behind a column. This time they knew where the vase was located, so they ran straight to the antechamber.

"THERE IT IS!"

Tim said, relieved that the vase still stood on its plinth among the offerings. He looked at it warily. "You don't think …"

"What?"

"Never mind." He was wondering whether Hercules might indeed be trapped inside, but even if he was, it made no difference to their mission. The best thing was to grab it and go as fast as possible.

Even so, that was easier said than done. The vase was big, bulky and heavy. If they needed to make a run for it ... "You take one end; I'll take the other," he said.

Together, Tim and Zoe hoisted the vase off its plinth and carried it between them. Tim tried very hard to carry it smoothly, just in case Hercules was actually trapped inside. He didn't want the great

hero to get motion sickness. Relief coming off them in waves, the children walked out of Hera's temple unchallenged.

"Down the stairs now … easy … easy …"

They were nearly at the bottom when they heard the peacocks' angry yowling.

Tim had no idea where the peacocks had come from. One moment there was no sign of them, and the next they flocked, yowling and growling, outside the entrance to Hera's temple. They seemed to materialize out of thin air. As if of one mind, the birds turned toward the children and charged in unison.

"YAH! RUN!"

Zoe cried, taking the temple steps two at a time.

"Careful – the vase," Tim said as it jiggled between them. It was hard to walk – let alone run – while carrying the heavy vessel.

"Don't worry about it. Let it smash. What does it matter?"

"What? No." Tim couldn't believe his ears and he tightened his grip on the handle. "Are you nuts?"

"At least that way Hera can't use it to trap Dad again."

She had a point, but Tim couldn't bring himself to break the vase deliberately. Something told him that would be a serious mistake.

"They're gaining on us," Zoe continued, "and it's slowing us down. Drop it."

"No. Wait. Put it down a sec." Tim had an idea. "The sunflower seeds!" His pockets were still full of the seeds they had picked in the gorgon's garden. He dug into his pockets and pulled out a handful. With a yell, he threw the food at the peacocks.

The yowling of the birds changed pitch as they looked at the unexpected treat. Heads twitching back and forth, beady eyes gleaming, the flock changed course and ran at the seeds. Soon they were pecking away as calmly and contentedly as a brood of chickens. Tim couldn't help smiling. It reminded him of a recent school trip, when his class had visited a farm.

"Here birdies, here birdies. Come and eat." He pulled out the sunflower blossom he had accidentally picked at the garden center and threw that to them as well.

"GREAT! CLEVER,"

Zoe said, resting her hands on her hips. "But we really ought to go before–"

It was too late. The goddess Hera, answering her pets' call, materialized among them in a golden haze. She didn't immediately spot the children. Instead, she

looked puzzled. "My petals. You're eating seeds – ugh, so common. Where did you get that food? Who gave it to you? Who's been feeding you without my permission?"

Hera's searching gaze found Tim and her cool blue eyes became chips of ice. "You! How did you get out of the labyrinth? How dare you presume to interfere with my birds?"

"Quick!" Nudging Zoe, Tim grasped the vase with both arms and cradled it against his chest.

As they stumbled down the last few steps, something went whizzing past them. Something small and round and like a baseball, but deep scarlet. Instinct made Tim want to reach out and catch it, but common sense – not to mention the heavy vase – stopped him. He barely had time to wonder what it was before it hit the ground near him. It exploded with an ear-splitting bang and what looked like hundreds of pieces of shrapnel

showered the air. Had the goddess just
thrown a hand grenade? Tim looked
back at Hera in disbelief, only to see
her holding another round object in her
hand. She was tossing it up and down
in her palm, clearly
preparing to lob it at
them.

"Pomegranate!"

Zoe shouted, her pupils dilating in fear. "Run faster."

Pomegranate? As in the fruit? Tim decided that this wasn't the right time to question what made sense and what didn't. They ran, ducking and weaving, as the blood-red fruit seeds exploded around them.

■ ■ ■

It wasn't until they'd reached the safety of Zoe's house, puffing and panting, that Tim felt able to raise the matter again.

"The pomegranate is Hera's sacred fruit," Zoe said, opening the front door and peering inside. "It's meant to symbolize fertility, but in her hands it becomes destructive. Like her peacocks. Hera turns everything into a weapon." She looked around furtively and raised a finger to her lips. "Now shush. Maybe Dad hasn't noticed we were gone."

"Zoe!" Hercules' voice boomed through the house and the walls shook. Zoe's shoulders slumped as her hope of slinking in unnoticed was shattered. The hero appeared before them, arms folded across his chest. "Where were you? Tim Baker, did you place my daughter in danger?"

"We took your vase back from Hera," Tim said, holding it out. "Zoe wanted to make sure it couldn't trap you again. She was trying to protect you."

Hercules scowled, his eyebrows meeting

in the middle of his forehead. "I told you, I don't need to be protected. I am the one that does the protecting around here, not the other way round. Have I made myself clear?"

Tim had never seen Hercules look so upset. "Y-yes, of course. We're sorry."

"Come along, dear – let the children in." Agatha appeared smoothly at her husband's elbow. She guided him away from the doorway and waved Tim and Zoe into the courtyard. Agatha took the vase away from Tim and looked at it with interest, her almond-shaped eyes narrowing as she read the ancient words.

"I'm starving," Zoe said, smiling prettily at her father. "Can we have lunch now?"

"LUNCH! HUMPH!

Your mother made the most wonderful
meal, but as you were gone I had to eat
it all myself. Even the rest of that honey
cake. There's nothing left."

"A piece of fruit will do."

Tim's stomach growled in agreement.
The sunflower seeds he'd eaten earlier
hadn't filled him up for long. "A quick
snack," he said. "I really need to go home.
Mom'll be upset. I've been gone for hours."

Hercules snorted and looked
meaningfully at Zoe. "Yes. I'm sure she is
worried. What good parent wouldn't be?"

"How will you get back?" Zoe asked,
twinkling at her father as she took
a handful of dried figs from a bowl.

She handed one to Tim, who devoured it hungrily.

"Not sure," he said, picking remnants of the sticky fruit out of his teeth. "I thought I could ask Hermes for a lift. He's how I came to be here in the first place, remember? I grabbed onto the vase as he flew away with it. Maybe he'll take me back, too. Mmm, yum, can I have another?"

"Are you sure you can trust him?" Zoe asked, handing over another couple of figs. "He serves Hera – he stole

the vase. If he sees
you, he might try to
take you back to her."

Tim shrugged. "Yes, but what else can I
do? I can't just catch a flight to Heathrow."

"A what to where?"

"Tim Baker," Agatha said, still holding the vase, "do you know what this says?"

"Zoe read some of it ..." he replied, wincing as Hercules shot Zoe a fierce look.

"He who holds me commands me," Agatha read out. She looked at Tim and her face broke into a brilliant smile. "What do you think that means?"

Tim looked at the vase doubtfully, trying to understand what Agatha was hinting at. She nodded and smiled, her eyes shining. An idea started to stir in his mind and he almost spat the fig out when the meaning of the words hit him.

"Hey! Does that mean I can use the vase to …"

"Oh yes!" Zoe cried, a grin splitting her face. "It must be! Don't you think so, Dad?"

She clutched her father's arm in delight.

"Maybe," Hercules mumbled, his eyes shifting left and right.

"It means I can command the vase to take me home, I think … I think it also means I can order it to bring me back." The more Tim thought about it, the more positive he became. He could use the vase to visit Ancient Greece any time he liked! All he had to do was command it: the magic vase was the key to time travel. *That* was why Hercules had kept the mysterious words a secret. He didn't want Tim getting himself or Zoe into danger. The hero gazed fixedly at the ground, not making eye contact.

Agatha nodded. "I think so too. But stay

for a proper meal first. I can whip something up."

As tempted as he was to try Ancient Greek food, Tim knew he had to hurry back home. "I'd better not. But thank you."

"Come back and see us again soon," Agatha said.

Nothing could have made Tim happier. Life at home would be unbearably dull after his adventure if this were the end. "Do you really think I can? Use the vase to come back, I mean?"

Agatha shrugged an elegant shoulder. "I don't see why not. Try it and see."

Tim glanced at Hercules, unsure of his reaction. Did he want Tim to come back or not?

"Yes, do return, my friend. But next time, be sure to not leave the house without me." Hercules engulfed Tim in a huge hug. One good thing about the hero was that he didn't stay angry for long. Zoe danced excitedly behind him.

Zoe hugged Tim too, taking the opportunity to whisper in his ear, "The crying statues. We've got to rescue them. Come back soon and we'll do it."

Tim nodded. Leaving Stheno's victims to their fate was his only regret about their adventure. He didn't know how he could possibly help, but there had to be a way. When he was released, Tim grasped the vase's handles and prepared himself for the flight.

"Oh vase," he said, feeling vaguely ridiculous, "take me home."

The thick golden mist that had obscured Tim when he'd first hitched a lift on the vase came back. It swirled around him, getting denser and denser, and he could feel himself being lifted off the ground.

"GOODBYE, EVERYONE,"

he called, gripping the big black handles for dear life. "I promise I'll come back one day … if I can …"

• • •

There was a soft thud as Tim hit the ground. He could feel carpet beneath his feet and as the golden mist evaporated his bedroom swam into focus. He was home! Feeling unsteady after the journey, he put the vase down carefully and waited for his head to stop spinning.

He didn't know how he was going to explain his long absence to his mother. She'd be sick with worry and likely more than a little angry. She might even have called the police! What on earth could he say? There was no way she'd believe the truth. Squaring his shoulders, Tim walked into the living room, ready to face her wrath. He expected to see her sitting there, face lined with worry, maybe even weeping …

Instead he could hear her humming cheerfully in the kitchen. It was the same tune she'd been humming many hours ago, when he'd first gone into his bedroom and checked on the vase. How could that be? Plates clattered and the smell of meat and garlic filled the air.

"Tim! Lunch," Mom called, as if he'd only just stepped out of the room.

Stunned, Tim glanced at the mantel clock. Only a few minutes had passed. The vase had brought him back mere moments after he'd left!

"COMING!"

He bustled into the kitchen, trying to act like nothing out of the ordinary had happened to him.

"Sit down," Mom ordered, then looked

at him strangely as he pulled out a chair. "What happened to your scarf?" she asked, pointing at it.

Tim looked at the ragged end where Theseus had tried to unravel it in a futile attempt to escape from Hera's labyrinth. "It, uh, came apart."

"I can see it came apart. How?"

"It's old. Guess it just crumbled," Tim said, thinking of Perseus' shield. He decided to change the subject before his mother asked more questions. "What's for lunch?"

"Your favorite. Ta-da!" With a flourish, Mom placed two heaping bowls of spaghetti bolognese on the table.

Tim stared at the coiled piles of pasta.

Long, thick, curly strands that wound and twisted their way around the bowl almost as if they were alive. They reminded him of the gorgon's hair-snakes and he gulped.

He'd just lost his appetite.

Look out for Tim's next ADVENTURE!

HOPELESS HEROES

ARACHNE'S GOLDEN GLOVES!

STELLA TARAKSON

Sweet Cherry
PUBLISHING

"Make sure you wear your scarf." Mom bustled into Tim's room as he finished getting dressed for school. Even though it was spring, she was wearing her winter coat. "It's freezing again. Wish I could just stay home today."

Tim wished she could too, or at least that she could be back when he returned from school. It wasn't much fun coming home to an empty house. It had felt even worse since his good friend Hercules had returned to his home in Ancient Greece.

"I can't. It's wrecked, remember?"

Mom hadn't believed Tim when he'd said that the scarf had unraveled itself. But what else could he say? She hadn't taken him seriously when he'd told her about Hercules, who'd been trapped in their old Greek vase by the wicked goddess Hera. Mom almost certainly wouldn't believe what had happened next. By grabbing onto the vase, Tim had unwittingly traveled to Hercules' home. Tim had been wearing the scarf at the time. It wasn't his fault it had got caught up in the action.

"That's right, I was going to get you

a new one. I forgot. Sorry, but I've had … uh … other things on my mind. Important things. Look, Tim, I've been meaning to talk to you about this. I shouldn't put it off any longer …" Mom's cheeks flushed red and a fine sheen of sweat covered her face.

Tim thought he knew what she wanted to say. He nodded and smiled reassuringly. "Is the furnace acting up again? Don't worry, Mom. Just call a man in."

Mom gulped and spluttered. "Funny you should say that. You see, I …" She cleared her throat, paused, and shook her head. "There isn't time for this now. I want to do it properly. How about you show me the scarf and I'll see if it's wearable?"

Tim handed it over and Mom frowned.

"No, it's too far gone. Toss it out. But put on your gloves at least."

"They're too small. Remember? You said you'd get a new pair."

Mom's face brightened. "Oh yes! Your grandma knitted you some. I'll go get them."

She left the scarf behind and Tim hastily crammed it in a drawer. He didn't want it thrown away. It was a souvenir of his adventure and a reminder of his encounter with Theseus the Minotaur Slayer. Theseus had unraveled the scarf in a futile attempt to escape the labyrinth that Hera had trapped them in. In the end, Tim had been the one to find the way out.

"Here." Mom came back in and handed him a pair of brown gloves. "Try them on."

They were much too big and were made out of coarse yarn.

"They're scratchy," Tim complained.

"They'll have to do for now," Mom said, fastening the belt on her coat. "I'm off. Make sure you wear them on your way to school. We don't want you getting chilblains again. Bye, dear."

She gave Tim a quick hug, left his room ... and screamed.

EEEE EEK!!

"What? What happened?" Tim bolted after her. He had never heard his mother scream like that before. It was a scream of sheer terror, as if there were a kill-you-with-a-glance gorgon after her.

"A sp-sp-spider …" Mom stuttered as she pointed at the wall. "Big."

Tim followed her shaking finger and, sure enough, a large spider was clambering along the hallway wall.

"Get a broom, quick! I'll keep watch to make sure it doesn't hide. Urgh!"

Tim darted down the corridor and came back with a broom, a glass and an envelope. He'd taken the opportunity to remove the scratchy brown gloves and thrust them in his jacket pocket.

"Whack it! Hard. Hurry before it jumps on us!"

Tim didn't want to hurt the spider, so he nudged it gently with the bristly end of the broom. It fell to the floor and his mother leaped back. Acting swiftly, Tim slapped the glass over it, taking care not to squash it.

"It's okay, Mom, I've caught it."

She shuddered. "Kill it! Urgh, it's horrible."

Tim looked down at the hairy brown

spider trapped in the glass, waving its long legs frantically as it tried to climb up the slippery sides. The poor thing hadn't done anything to hurt them. It was just crawling along, minding its own business. He couldn't bring himself to kill it.

"I'll take it outside," he said, bending down and sliding the envelope under the glass.

"Don't you dare. It'll come back inside. Just … squish it or something."

Tim had never realized his mother had such a vicious streak. He flashed her a severe look. "I'll take it down the street and let it go. It won't come back." Not after hearing his mother scream like that. The poor spider was probably scarred for life.

"It better not," Mom grumbled. She leaned forward to kiss him like she usually did, then backed away nervously. "See you tonight. And then we've got to talk."

Tim carried the spider to the end of the street, being careful not to jolt it. The spider stared up at him through the glass, bright eyes gleaming.

Tim rather liked the idea of keeping it as a pet but knew his mother would go nuts. "Sorry about this," he murmured. "Nothing personal." The spider waved its front legs as if it understood.

"Talking to a glass now, are ya, Cinderella? Next you'll be talking to a teacup." It was Leo the bully, who seemed to have made it his life's mission to make Tim miserable. The unkind nickname was a jab at the fact that Tim had to help out with housework.

Tim and Leo had crossed paths the day before, when they had both been dragged around a boring garden center. Leo had tripped Tim and Tim had returned the favor. It had felt good at the time. Great, actually. But now that they were alone in an empty street, with Leo clenching his beefy fists, Tim thought it probably wasn't the wisest thing he could have done. If only Hercules were still with him, he'd frighten Leo off again. But no.

This time, Tim was on his own.

"How about I smash that stupid glass?" Leo said, thrusting his freckly face close to Tim's. "Or maybe I should smash your stupid nose instead. Whaddya reckon?"

Tim thrust the glass near the bully's face. "How do you like my new pet? I was taking it for a walk before school."

Leo recoiled, his face aghast, before quickly recovering his composure. Hands on hips, he put on an I-don't-care expression. "It's all right. I s'pose." He sniffed, but eyed the glass with respect. "What sort of spider is he?"

"Actually it's a she. The females are

bigger than males. And more dangerous."
Tim had no idea what type of spider
it was, but using his imagination had
never been a problem for him.
Guessing that Leo wouldn't
know anyway, Tim invented
something impressively
dangerous. "She's an
Australian howling widow
spider. They're called that
because they howl after
a kill. See her powerful
fangs?" He thrust the
glass closer and Leo
blinked.

"Is ... is she deadly?"

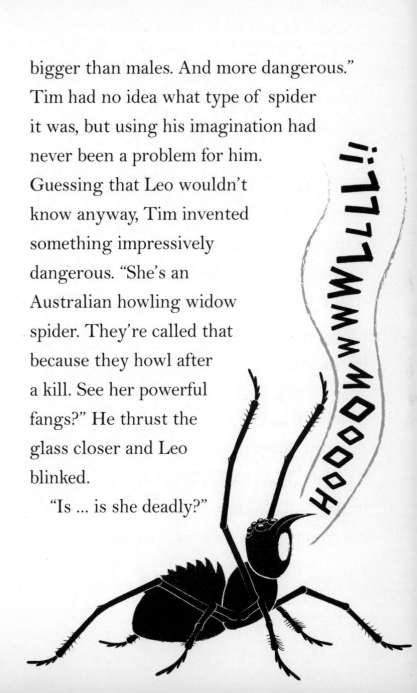

"Of course. But that's okay. I've trained her not to bite my friends."

Leo's eyes widened. "What's her name?"

Tim said the first thing that came to mind. "Hera." It seemed fitting to name her after the dangerous goddess who had trapped him in the labyrinth.

"Do you often take her for walks?"

"I try. She gets restless if I don't. Last week she killed a rat because she was bored."

Leo took an involuntary step backward. "Dude, have you ever thought of getting something normal? Like a dog or a cat?"

"Nah." Tim shook his head. As much as he'd love a real pet, he knew they couldn't afford one. Still, he wasn't about to admit that to Leo. "Hera would get jealous and kill it."

Leo blanched, which made the freckles on his face stand out more clearly. "Can ... can I hold her?"

Tim couldn't help feeling a grudging respect for the bully. Most kids would turn and flee. Whatever else could be said about Leo, there was no doubting his courage. "Sure. Hold the envelope under the glass, or she'll climb on your arm."

Gulping, Leo held out his hands. They were shaking and Tim could see the effort the bully put into steadying them. He also noticed how swollen his fingers were. Purplish red and raw, the skin was pulled tight over the knuckles. It was even blistered in places. "What's wrong with your hands?"

Leo's expression instantly hardened. "Nothing." He stepped away and thrust his hands behind his back.

Tim thought he knew. Chilblains. He often got them in winter, but nowhere near as badly as Leo. Maybe that was because Mom made Tim wear gloves when he left the house. He wondered why Leo wasn't wearing any.

Balancing the glass and envelope carefully with

one hand, Tim reached into his jacket pocket and pulled out the scratchy brown gloves his grandmother had knitted. He shrugged and held them up. "Here. These are too big for me."

Competing expressions chased each other across the bully's face. Anger, embarrassment, gratitude. Resentment. He stared at the gloves, lips pressed into a thin, hard line, and didn't move.

"Go on, take them." Tim waggled them in the air.

"I don't want them."

Leo opened his mouth to reply, but the words died on his lips. Not meeting Tim's eye, he snatched the gloves and stalked off in the direction of their school.

Tim watched until Leo was out of sight before placing his pretend pet on the footpath. "I have to let you go now," he said to the spider, lifting off the glass. "Sorry to bring you out in the cold, but you know what mothers are like. It's better than being squashed, though."

The spider agreed. It reared up on its hind legs and waved its front legs, enjoying the feel of fresh air on its fangs. Its bright eyes sparkled in the morning light, and Tim thought he detected gratitude in its gaze. It was staring up at him as if he were a hero.

A lump formed in Tim's throat. He didn't feel like a hero ... not since he'd left the gorgon's victims to their fate. Since returning from Ancient Greece yesterday, Tim couldn't stop thinking of the people the gorgon had turned to stone. He wished he could go back and help them.

Maybe he could! A spell written on the old Greek vase suggested that Tim could

order it to take him anywhere. It had certainly worked when he'd commanded it to bring him home after his recent adventure. But that had been in Greece, where the vase's magic might have been stronger. Would it work here, too? Could he order the vase to take him back to Ancient Greece? There was only one way to find out.

The spider turned and scuttled under a shrub as Tim ran back home, his fingers crossed.

HOPELESS HEROES

To download Hopeless Heroes

ACTIVITIES
AND
POSTERS

visit:
www.sweetcherrypublishing.com/resources

Sweet
Cherry
PUBLISHING